DOWNTOWN DINOSAURS
DINOSAUR OLYMPICS

JEANNE WILLIS

Illustrated by Arthur Robins

Piccadilly Press • London

For Dad,
who is now extinct but delighted in dinosaurs.
J. W.

For Ollie
A.R.

First published in Great Britain in 2012
by Piccadilly Press Ltd,
5 Castle Road, London NW1 8PR
www.piccadillypress.co.uk

Text copyright © Jeanne Willis, 2012
Illustrations copyright © Arthur Robins, 2012

A catalogue record for this book is available
from the British Library

ISBN: 978 1 84812 240 6

3 5 7 9 10 8 6 4 2

Printed and bound by CPI Group (UK) Ltd, Croydon, CR0 4YY
Cover design by Simon Davis
Cover illustration by Arthur Robins

DOWNTOWN DINOSAURS

One of the funniest authors for children, Jeanne Willis has been writing since she was five and is the author of many children's books including *Tadpole's Promise*, *Who's in the Loo* and *Bottoms Up* and the hugely popular *Dr Xargle* series.

She has won numerous awards including the Smarties Prize, the Red House Children's Book Award and the Sheffield Children's Book Award.

An enormously popular cartoonist and illustrator, Arthur Robins has illustrated best-selling books by Laurence Anholt, Martin Waddell and Michael Rosen, including *Little Rabbit Foo Foo*, and has even produced some stamps for the Royal Mail.

Downtown Dinosaurs:

Dinosaur Olympics
Dinosaurs in Disguise *(coming soon)*

CHAPTER 1

PARTY TIME

If there was one thing the Uptown Dinosaurs liked more than anything, it was a good party. Which was the perfect invitation for some rotten beast to come and ruin it.

It had all started off so well. The Stigsons had sent out the invitations and their neighbours in

Fossil Street had been looking forward to the big bash at the stegosauruses' place for weeks.

It was Uncle Loops's one hundred and ninetieth birthday – a ripe old age even for a sauropod and a great excuse for a celebration. Although his brain had shrunk from the size of a walnut to the size of a peanut during the late cretaceous period, and he had no idea which era it was let alone which day, his family wanted this to be a party even he wouldn't forget.

Mrs Stigson was busy putting candles on his gigantic birthday cake when she was interrupted. 'One hundred and eighty-two, one hundred and eighty-three . . .'

KNOCK! KNOCK!

'Oh, fossils! Now I've lost count. Daaarwiiiin! Get the door, son. Our guests are arriving.'

'Can't Dad answer it?' yelled Darwin. 'I'm in the bog.'

'I'll get it,' wheezed Uncle Loops, plodding towards the door with his zimmer frame. Halfway across the hall, he stopped. 'What was it I was getting again?'

KNOCK! KNOCK!

'I'll go,' said Mr Stigson, who was on his knees sorting out the karaoke machine. 'It'll be the next millennium by the time he gets there.'

'Be nice to him, Maurice. It's his birthday,' said Mrs Stigson.

'Is it?' beamed Uncle Loops. 'Again?'

KNOCK! KNOCK!

Uncle Loops frowned. 'Who's there?' he called. 'Is it care in the community?'

'No, it's Mrs Merrick,' boomed a voice.

'Mrs Merrick who?'

Mr Stigson opened the door. 'Ah, Phyllis. Do come in. You remember Phyllis Merrick, don't you, Uncle Loops? She's the mastodon from number four.'

Uncle Loops looked her up and down quizzically and slapped his forehead. 'Oh yes. Fat Phyllis – that *is* what we call her in this house, isn't it?'

Mrs Merrick let out a long, disapproving snort through her trunk.

'His hearing is not what it was,' said Mr Stigson hastily as he led her to the kitchen. 'Goodness, you look so trim, what we actually call you is *Fit* Phyllis.'

There was another knock at the door and Mrs Stigson called out, 'Will someone *please* answer that? I bet it's Fat Phyllis. She's always the first to arrive and the last to leave.'

'I have half a mind to be the first to leave!' muttered Mrs Merrick, huffily.

'You have half a mind? That's twice as much as me,' said Uncle Loops. 'Thank goodness I still have my memory. I'll see you out. You turning up out of the blue like this, anyone would think it was my birthday.'

But when the matronly mastodon saw the buffet table groaning with more vegetarian delights than a hippy's delicatessen, she decided to stay.

'What a marvellous spread, Mrs Stigson,' she said, hoovering up a plate of vol-au-vents.

'You can call me Lydia,' said Mrs Stigson.

'Very well, Lydia,' said Phyllis. 'And you can call me Mrs Merrick.'

Darwin, who had been left to greet the second guest, announced his arrival. 'Mum, Sir . . . Thingy is here.'

'Sir Tempest Stratford, darlings!' boomed the triceratops, trotting into the centre of the room. 'You may have seen me in my latest film, *Planet of the Grapes* . . . Now where's the birthday boy?'

'I have no idea,' said Uncle Loops.

As the other guests arrived, Mrs Stigson steered Sir Tempest over to the karaoke machine and gave him a glass of champagne and a list of songs.

'Would you like to start us off with "The Birdy Song"?' she said. 'I know you're used to being on the stage.'

The triceratops gave her a long, hard stare. 'I'll have to ask my agent. I'm auditioning for a musical tomorrow. I'm playing the part of the Fartful Stodger and I don't want to ruin my vocal cords.'

'Yes or no, Sir Tempest?' said Mrs Stigson, fiddling with her cocktail cherry. 'I've got some lovely old tunes here . . . "Let's Get it On", "Do You Think I'm Sexy?" . . .'

Sir Tempest almost choked on a cheesy puff. He looked around to make sure Mr Stigson wasn't listening and lowered his voice to a whisper. 'I do find you oddly attractive but I didn't think it was *that* sort of a party.'

'Ooh, Sir Tempest!' giggled Mrs Stigson. 'Those are the song titles, silly.'

Blushing from his horny frill to his feet, he swept off to rescue Mrs Merrick's hat which had been knocked into a vat of trifle by Frank and Ernest – twin ankylosaurs – who fancied

themselves as swashbuckling types and were fencing with cucumbers.

'Great party, Uncle,' grinned Darwin, swinging the old stegosaurus around to the vibes of Jurassic Jazz.

'Whose is it? Anyone we know?' asked Loops. 'I hear the mayor's coming. Whoever's birthday it is, they must be pretty important.'

'They are to me,' said Darwin.

Uncle Loops had been Darwin's favourite relative since he was a hatchling and the two of them got on like a house on fire – especially the time when Uncle Loops found that bumper box of matches.

Having spoken to his wife, Mr Stigson marched over to Sir Tempest and cornered him by a rubber plant.

'I want a word with you, Stratford.'

'Maurice, before you say anything, I wasn't

flirting with Mrs Stigson,' said Sir Tempest, flustered. 'The champagne went straight to my horns. It was a complete misunderstanding.'

Mr Stigson looked confused. 'What was?'

'Nothing. Nothing at all,' said Tempest, realising he'd got away with it. 'What was it you wanted, dear boy – my autograph?'

'I was going to ask you a favour, actually,' said Mr Stigson. 'I was wondering if you'd say a few words after the mayor has presented Uncle Loops with his birthday gift.'

Sir Tempest gave a sharp intake of breath. 'A few words? Words don't come cheap, you know.'

'Mum, Boris is here!' called Darwin, interrupting them.

The mayor shot down their front path and screeched to a halt on his bike, his robe blowing out behind him, making him look like a mad caped crusader.

'Hello, hellay, no need to bow and scrape,' he blustered as he moved among the guests. 'Let's jolly well get on with the presentation, shall we? Where's the watch? I know I put it somewhere no one would think to look . . . Ah, here it is, tucked inside my cycling briefs. It's all right, Mrs Merrick, they're clean on.'

'I expect that makes a pleasant change,' grunted Mrs Merrick. 'Even so, you might have put it in a gift box.'

Boris shook his head. 'Cut-backs. Blame the last government. Now, where is Mr Augustus Luperton? Hate to hurry you but I've got three awards down my undercrackers due for delivery and they're playing havoc with my doodahs.'

'Has any one seen Uncle Loops?' called Mrs Stigson. 'Darwin, can you please go and find him? Quickly, the mayor is a busy man.'

Loops was having a snooze in the wardrobe, so Darwin spoke to him through the keyhole.

'Wake up, Uncle. The mayor wants to give you a special present.' 'My birthday's not for ages,' yawned Uncle Loops from underneath a pile of moth-eaten fur coats. 'It's today,' said Darwin. 'You're one hundred and ninety years old today.'

Uncle Loops stumbled out and rubbed his eyes. 'One hundred and ninety? Jeepers, how long have I been asleep?'

Darwin helped him into the stair lift and sat on his lap while they rode down. As they landed in the hall, Boris was ready and waiting.

'I give you Boris the mayor!' announced Sir Tempest with a theatrical flourish. 'That's six words at a fiver each. You owe me forty quid, Maurice.'

'You've just eaten your own weight in chocolate brownies, Stratford,' said Mr Stigson. 'Cocoa costs more than words. Throw in a speech and we're quits, I reckon.'

'Mr Luperton, you old devil!' said the mayor, shaking Uncle Loops so vigorously by the foot that his dentures rattled. 'I believe congratulations are in order.'

'Why?' said Uncle Loops. 'What have you done?'

'Me?' said Boris. 'I haven't done anything. This is all about you, sir!'

'Who, sir?' said Uncle Loops.

'It might be quicker if you just gave him the you-know-what,' said Mrs Stigson.

The mayor handed the solid gold gift to Uncle Loops, who seemed genuinely pleased with it.

'Thanks, Brian. It's a compass, right? I've always wanted one of those,' he said. 'For one dreadful minute I thought it was going to be a watch.'

'Speech!' cried the guests. 'Speech!'

'I . . .' began Uncle Loops, but before he could say anything, Sir Tempest thrust himself forward.

'My cue! Maurice has asked me to say a few words . . .'

'Booooo!' heckled the guests.

Sir Tempest took no notice and continued. 'Firstly, I would like to say that the hay and horseradish sandwiches were particularly . . .'

He was interrupted by someone rapping loudly on the front door.

'Hooray!' cheered the guests.

KNOCK! KNOCK!

There it was again.

'Who can that be at this time of night?' wondered Mrs Stigson. 'Everyone with an invitation is here already.'

A hush fell over the room. Even Sir Tempest Stratford kept his mouth shut and Mrs Merrick twitched the curtains nervously.

'Get away from the window, Phyllis,' whispered Mr Stigson. 'Everybody duck down.'

'Who are we hiding from, Dad?' asked Darwin. 'Is it the Downtown Dinosaurs?'

Mr Stigson tried in vain to disguise the note of terror that had crept into his voice. 'Shhh, Darwin! I thought I told you never to say the d-word!'

Chapter 2

Postman's Knock?

The dinosaurs held their breath, praying that whoever was at the door would get bored and go away, but no ...

Knock! Knock!

Mrs Merrick was having palpitations. Sir Tempest was so scared, he relieved himself in the rubber plant. Even the rosy-cheeked mayor had gone a whiter shade of pale.

Little wonder. As far back as anyone could remember, there had been bloody battles between the Downtown Dinosaurs who were carnivores and the Uptown Dinosaurs who were herbivores. Unfortunately, most of the blood spilt belonged to the mild-mannered herbivores who lived in the neighbourhood around Fossil Street. At one time or another, all of them had been sworn at, mugged or lost a relative to a deinosuchus or tyrannosaurus from Raptor Road.

'They're dreadful sports,' muttered Boris. 'They come over here, destroying our way of life. I'd have them lined up against a wall and shot.'

'Oh, there speaks a true, peace-loving vegan,' mocked Sir Tempest. 'I'm surprised at you, Boris, you old edmontonia.'

'I've tried to be reasonable,' insisted Boris. 'Remember my policy of involving them in team games so we could bond? That backfired somewhat, didn't it? My eyes still water when I remember where they shoved that cricket ball . . .'

'Shush, they'll hear us,' whispered Mrs Stigson.

'Who will?' shouted Uncle Loops. 'Why is everybody whispering?'

'Darwin, please control your uncle,' squeaked Sir Tempest. 'He'll get us killed.'

KNOCK! KNOCK!

Everybody scattered and while it looked as if they were playing a game of Sardines, they were really squeezing into ridiculously cramped places to save their hides.

'You're sitting on my bonnet, Sir Tempest!' muttered Mrs Merrick, struggling for breath behind the sofa.

Tempest Stratford shifted his buttocks. 'I'm sorry, my dear. I didn't realise you had it on.'

Even Frank and Ernest, the feisty ankylosaur twins, had taken fright and were squashed together like a pair of prickly giant chestnuts in the cupboard under the stairs.

Darwin refused to join them. By some evolutionary quirk, he was more intelligent than the average stegosaurus and he'd sussed that whoever was at the door was no carnivore – the knocking had the wrong rhythm altogether.

If it had been a T. Rex or a deinosuchus, it would have made an aggressive *rappety-rap*. Besides, after a few knocks, they would have just booted the door down.

By Darwin's calculations, whoever was at the door was small – quite a lot smaller than him by the sounds of it – possibly a cute little creature such as a hapalops or an dinohippus who had become domesticated and gone astray.

KNOCK! KNOCK!

As his parents were too busy hiding to stop him, Darwin tiptoed over to the door and opened it a tiny crack. There was nobody there. Darwin shrugged and went inside.

'Whoever it was, they've gone,' he announced cheerily. 'Let's party!'

He turned the music back up and gradually, the guests crawled out of their hiding places.

'Let's play Spin the Bottle,' said Mrs Stigson brightly. 'Everyone sit in a circle.'

'How does this game go?' wondered Uncle Loops.

'You spin the bottle and if it points to Mrs Merrick, you can give her a kiss,' Mrs Stigson explained.

Uncle Loops looked in horror as the middle-aged mastodon puckered up. 'Count me out!'

KNOCK! KNOCK!

The guests exchanged nervous glances. Whoever was knocking really knew how to kill the atmosphere.

'I'm fed up with this,' groaned Darwin. 'It's not like Uncle Loops is one hundred and ninety every day.'

'Don't open the door without looking, Darwin,' warned Mrs Stigson. 'Your brother did and that's why you're now an only child.'

Confident that it wasn't a carnivore, Darwin took no notice and answered it. Again, he could see nobody on the step, but there was a long piece of tatty string tied to the knocker which trailed around the side of the house. Darwin followed it and on the other end of the string, hiding behind the corner with his rabid pet cynognathus was . . .

'The australopithecus! Mum, Ozzi's playing tricks on us again!' yelled Darwin.

The tiny, hairy sub-human bared its teeth, pulled the string as hard as it could and made the knocker bang again. It was clearly delighted with its new invention and seemed very keen to show it off.

Mrs Stigson came outside and clapped her hands to scare it away. 'Shoo! Off you go, Ozzi, and take Nogs with you. And you can scoop his mess up before you go. I'm sick and tired of him doing his business on my doorstep.'

The australopithecus jiggled his thumbs in his ears and skittered off with his pet snapping at his heels.

'I might have guessed,' said Mrs Merrick when she heard who was responsible for putting them in fear of their lives. 'If I ever catch him, I'll slap his bottom. I'm sick of his practical jokes. I bet it was him who stole my smalls off the washing line, the little monkey.'

'Must have needed a truck to shift 'em!' chortled Uncle Loops.

'But he isn't a monkey, is he?' said Mr Stigson seriously. 'I'm afraid Ozzi is higher up the evolutionary scale than we give him credit for – I wouldn't want to mess with him.'

'Lighten up, Maurice,' scoffed Sir Tempest as

he tucked into the crisps. 'Australopithecus is an insignificant little species. They'll die out in a few years. They may totter about on two legs like they own the place but they're hardly going to rule the world.'

Everybody laughed. Then suddenly the room was plunged in darkness.

'Is it bedtime? Oh good,' said Uncle Loops.

'Ozzi's at it again,' moaned the mayor. 'Now he's fiddling with the lights.'

But it was only Mrs Stigson switching the lights off so everyone could enjoy the candles on Uncle Loops's cake. There were a lot more than one hundred and ninety because she'd lost count and they were becoming a major contribution to global warming.

'Augustus, blow them out before I get heat stroke,' gasped Mrs Merrick, fanning herself with a napkin.

'I'm not sure I've got the puff,' panted Uncle Loops. 'Someone help me out. How about you, Sir Compost? You're full of wind.'

Sir Tempest considered the matter for a while as the candles melted down to stubs and coated the cake with a thick layer of wax. 'Well,' he said, 'if I were to blow out your candles, I'd regard that as a professional performance. I'm afraid you'll have to call my agent.'

'I'm afraid I'll have to call the fire brigade if you hang around much longer,' said Mr Stigson. 'Fancy trying to take advantage of an old age pensioner.'

'Blame the last government!' bellowed Boris.

'I'll help you, Uncle,' said Darwin. 'Make a birthday wish on three. One, two, three!'

Uncle Loops shut his eyes and blew. 'I wish it wasn't my birthday.'

His guests cheered and broke into song:

'Happy birthday to Loops!

'Happy birthday to Loops!

'Happy birthday, Augustus,

'Happy birthday to Loops!'

As the party poppers went off and the suffocating whiff of candle smoke choked the guests, Mrs Stigson cut the cake.

'Just a small piece, please,' said Mrs Merrick. 'No, not that small. A bit bigger, dear. Bigger . . .

bigger . . . That's it, just cut the cake in half. That'll do me.'

Darwin scraped the candle wax off his own slice and was just about to bite into it when Sir Tempest banged on the table with the ladle from the punch bowl.

'Someone at the door. I'll get it,' said Uncle Loops.

Darwin sat him back down. 'It's only Sir Tempest trying to get our attention. I'm afraid he's going to make another speech.'

'Be afraid,' groaned Uncle Loops. 'Be very afraid.'

Sir Tempest cleared his throat. 'Everybody sitting comfortably? Splendid, then I will finish my lovely speech that

was so rudely interrupted earlier —'

'Boo!' interrupted the guests.

'And I can only hope,' he continued, 'that this time, nobody knocks at the door, because I should very much like to say that the hay and horseradish baps provided by our delightful hostess were absolutely —'

KNOCK! KNOCK!

'Hooray!' cheered the audience. 'Hooray for Ozzi! Good timing!'

Sir Tempest put his hands on his hips and rolled his eyes. 'Really, I don't know why I bother.'

'Carry on, Stratford,' said Mr Stigson, refreshing the speaker's glass of champagne. 'It's only Ozzi, ignore him. He'll soon go away.'

'Dad?' asked Darwin.

Sir Tempest had a quick swig and tried to pick up from where he'd left off. 'Before I propose a toast to our dear friend Augustus, I would just like to say, if you'd give me a flaming chance, that I thought the hay and horserad—'

Knock! Knock! Knock!

'Ignore it,' said Mr Stigson. 'Ozzi's toying with you.'

'Dad!' said Darwin urgently, realising the knocks did not sound the same as before.

Sir Tempest slammed his glass down and narrowed his eyes. 'I'm sorry, I can't ignore it, Maurice. I'm a professional, I'm going to give that little beggar a piece of my mind.'

'Can I have a piece?' piped Uncle Loops.

'But Sir Tempest —' started Darwin.

Ignoring whatever it was Darwin had to say, the triceratops strode over to the door, flung it open and bellowed, 'I've had just about enough of you, you bandy-legged, flea-bitten little half-wit!'

But it was not the australopithecus.

And it wasn't a carnivore.

It was *three* carnivores.

Three of the meanest-looking carnivores that ever roamed the earth: a mad pteranodon, a deadly deinosuchus and their leader – a terrifying tyrannosaurus rex who already had his great big foot through the door.

'Where's my party bag?' roared Flint Beastwood.

Chapter 3

Musical Thumps

'I hear there's a party,' growled Flint Beastwood, cupping his ear hole with his monstrous sickle-shaped claws and clicking them to the music. 'Our invitations must have got lost in the post, lads. What do you reckon, Terry?'

The pteranodon hunched himself up like a hideous leather duffel bag and displayed a row of teeth that wouldn't have looked out of place on a chainsaw.

'I don't think this miserable bunch of celery-suckers invited us at all, boss.'

'Oh dear, oh dear,' said Beastwood, dabbing at his eyes. 'That's hurt my feelings something rotten. I'm welling up.'

As the rest of the guests backed up against a wall, Mr Stigson did his best to explain. 'I'm sure I sent your invites. Ozzi must have fished them out of the postbox.'

'He does it all the time,' added Mrs Stigson. 'He's looking for money tucked inside birthday cards. More to be pitied than scolded really.'

The deinosuchus cracked his knuckles, lifted a thunderous thigh and aimed his huge foot in the direction of the door. 'Want me to kick it in, boss?'

Flint Beastwood stroked his chin thoughtfully. 'Not necessary, Mr Cretaceous. I think you'll find it's already open.'

All three of them barged their way past Sir Tempest Stratford, who bravely, or stupidly, tried to block their path. 'I'm sorry, you can't come in without a tie, Mr Beastwood. This is a very posh do. The mayor's here . . . somewhere.'

'He's behind the curtains,' said Uncle Loops helpfully.

Mr Cretaceous whisked them back so hard they flew off the end of the rails.

'Boris, me old mate,' said Beastwood, looking the mayor up and down. What are you doing behind there? Anyone would think you're trying to avoid me.'

'Playing Hide and Seek,' cringed Boris. 'Well done, you found me . . . your turn.'

The tyrannosaurus rex gave a sinister smile. 'You want to play games, do you? I like playing games. What shall we play, lads?'

'How about Musical Thumps?' said Mr Cretaceous.

Boris looked hopeful for a second. 'That sounds

rather jolly,' he said. 'I'm not sure we've ever played that one.'

'What do we have to do?' asked Mrs Merrick.

Flint Beastwood went over to the karaoke machine. 'Simple. Everybody stand in the middle of the room — that's it, make a herd — that includes you, Mrs Merrick.'

'Dad, I really don't think we should play this game,' whispered Darwin.

'Just humour them,' said Mr Stigson. 'If you can't beat 'em, join 'em.'

Flint Beastwood must have overheard and nodded at him. 'Beat them? Yes, I see you've played this game before, Maurice.'

'That's not fair,' tutted Frank and Ernest, the competitive ankylosaurs. 'That means he'll probably win.'

'It's not the winning,' said Flint Beastwood, 'it's the taking apart. Are we all ready?'

'Ready, boss,' drooled Terry O'Dactyl, circling the terrified guests.

'Me too!' said Boris, keen to keep him sweet. 'What do we do next, Mr Beastwood?'

'Didn't I say? Silly me.' The tyrannosaurus slapped his own wrist playfully. 'When I turn the music up, all you have to do is stand still while we beat you to a pulp.' 'Musical Thumps, geddit?' said Mr Cretaceous, spitting out a lizard that was stuck in his teeth.

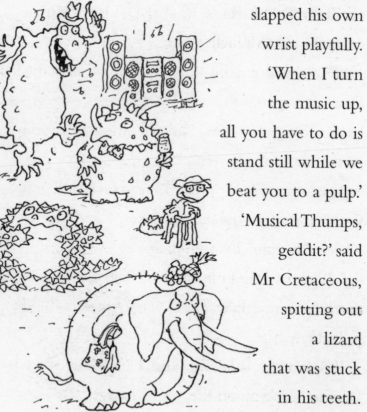

As Flint turned the music up, the deinosuchus tanked towards the horrified herbivores.

'I'm not standing for this,' said Mrs Merrick.

'So sit down!' roared Beastwood.

Out of the corner of his eye, Darwin could see Terry O'Dactyl creeping up on Uncle Loops, who seemed to think the fight had been laid on as part of the entertainment and was shouting encouragement. 'Gahn! Hit him! I was hoping for some dancing girls but this boxing match isn't so bad.'

'Look out, Uncle!' shouted Darwin, jumping on the

pteranodon's bony back and trying to wrestle him off.

'Maurice, do something!' shrieked Mrs Stigson.

'Boris, do something!' gargled Mr Stigson as Mr Cretaceous pinned him down by the throat.

Boris grabbed the punch ladle and banged it repeatedly on the table.

'Don't tell me there's another speech,' groaned Uncle Loops.

'Order . . . Order!' yelled Boris.

Uncle Loops brightened up. 'Are we having a take-away? I'll have beansprouts and a portion of egg-fried rice.'

Boris hit the table again. 'Stop it, chaps!' he bellowed. 'This just isn't cricket!'

Mr Cretaceous helped himself to the tomatoes and bowled them at Boris's head. 'Howzat!'

'I'm serious!' said Boris, wiping the pips

from his face with a napkin. 'You can throw whatever you like at us, but —'

The carnivores from Raptor Road pelted him with a selection of savoury snacks, then he carried on regardless.

'As mayor, I'd like us to find a way to live in peace and suggest we start by enjoying a non-violent communal activity. Tennis, perhaps? How does that grab you, Mr Beastwood?'

Flint got hold of Boris's nose and squeezed it tightly. 'How does that grab *you*, Mr Mayor?'

'Will you please just go!' cried Mrs Stigson. 'What have we ever done to you? You're upsetting Uncle Loops.'

'Upsetting Uncle Loops? I'm not best pleased myself,' spluttered Boris through clamped nostrils.

Beastwood released his grip and stroked Mrs Stigson's cheek. 'I'm a sucker for a pretty face,' he said. 'You're a lucky man, Mr Stigson. I tell you what I'll do. I'm going to call my boys off and we'll go home nice and quietly.'

'Thank you,' said Mr Stigson.

'I'll show you to the door – what's left of it.'

The tyrannosaurus shook his head. 'Not so hasty, Maurice. Before I go, you must pay your party tax.'

'Party tax?' said Mr Stigson. 'What party tax?'

'It's the law,' said Flint. 'Claws ten, paragraph six. If you have a party to which the citizens of Raptor Road are not invited, you have to pay me – isn't that right Mr Mayor?'

'It's a new one on me,' said Boris, scratching his head. 'How much is it?'

Flint Beastwood made a great show of doing the arithmetic in his head and told him.

Mr Stigson gave a sharp intake of breath. 'I haven't got that kind of money. Stratford, I don't suppose you could lend me a couple of . . .'

Sir Tempest shook his head vigorously. 'I'm that skint I've resorted to doing adverts.'

'The law is the law,' shrugged Flint, poking

around in Mrs Stigson's knick-knacks. 'If you haven't got the readies, I'll just have to take something of value.'

'Just as well he doesn't know about my new compass, Darwin,' shouted Uncle Loops, dangling his new gold watch by its chain.

'Put it away, Uncle,' whispered Darwin.

But the beady eyes of the tyrannosaurus had already spotted it. 'I'll have that, thank you.'

'It's not yours!' said Darwin, trying to grab it. 'Give it back.'

Flint Beastwood laughed in his face and jerked it out of reach. 'Eat spinach, Shorty. You want to teach your lad some manners, Stigson.'

With that, he swept the champagne glasses off the table, clicked his fingers and stomped out of the house, closely followed by his loathsome sidekicks.

As soon as the carnivores had gone, the guests made their excuses and left.

'Don't all rush off,' said Mrs Stigson. 'We were going to have a sing-song.'

'I have to go to my exercise class,' said Mrs Merrick. 'It's Bums and Tums tonight.'

'We've got to revise for our exams,' lied Frank and Ernest.

The only one who had a good excuse to leave was the mayor, who needed to deliver awards.

Mr Stigson reached into the drinks cabinet. 'You'll stay, won't you, Stratford?'

'My agent just called,' said Sir Tempest. 'I must rehearse my audition for *Jurassic Pork*. I'd better dash, cheery-bye!'

Mrs Stigson looked around at the mess and sighed. The curtains lay crumpled on the floor, there were burst tomatoes stuck to the wall and there was glass everywhere.

'Looks like someone had a great party,' said Uncle Loops.

'I'll get the mop,' groaned Mrs Stigson. 'Can you give me a hand, Darwin?'

As Darwin picked the coleslaw and crushed crisps out of the carpet, he felt very angry. He was sick of being threatened by carnivores. To have eaten his brother was bad enough but to be called Shorty in front of everybody was total humiliation.

'Has anybody seen my compass?' hollered Uncle Loops from the toilet. 'I need it to find my way out of the bathroom.'

Darwin put down the dustpan and brush. How dare Flint Beastwood take his Uncle's watch!

'That does it,' he announced. 'Mum, I'm going out.'

Just as he was about to leave, his father stopped him. 'Where do you think you're going, son? It's dark out there.'

Darwin looked his father in the eye. 'I'm going Downtown, to Raptor Road.'

Mr Stigson stood in front of him so he couldn't get past. 'No, Darwin. I can't allow it. You'll be eaten alive.'

'Dad, I have to do this. Someone has to stand up to Beastwood – if you won't, I will!'

Darwin tried to dive through his father's legs, but Mr Stigson grabbed him by the shoulders.

'I've tried. My father tried, my grandfather tried, generations of Stigsons have tried to make peace with the carnivores but it's not in their nature. They're the hunters, we're the hunted. We have to live with it.'

'I don't want to,' said Darwin.

'We'll see what your mother has to say about that, shall we . . . Lydia?'

Mrs Stigson ran in looking flustered.

'Have either of you seen Uncle Loops?'

'He was in the bathroom,' said Darwin.

'He's not now. I've looked everywhere. He didn't go out, did he?'

'I don't know,' said Mr Stigson. 'But what's the panic? He's always wandering off. He'll be back when he's hungry.'

But Darwin wasn't so sure. A dreadful thought crossed his mind. 'What if he's gone to get his watch back off Flint Beastwood?'

Mrs Stigson threw her hands up in the air and let out a mournful moo.

'Noooo! We can't lose another Stigson, especially not on his birthday. Somebody do something!'

CHAPTER 4

THE MEAT MARKET

'I'll go after Uncle Loops,' said Darwin. 'He can't have got far on his zimmer frame. If I take my bike, I'll catch up with him long before he gets to Raptor Road.'

Before his dad could stop him, he was out the door. He ran to the bicycle shed and jumped on the saddle. But as he went to pedal off, the bike bucked like a bronco and threw him over the handlebars into a bush. He examined the bike and shouted in frustration.

'The australopithecus! Why me, why now?'

Ozzi had obviously been at it again – he'd removed the back wheel and replaced it with a square one. Whether he needed the round wheel for one of his inventions or swapped it as a joke, Darwin didn't know or care; the bike was useless. The buses weren't running either – the night shift only had a skeleton crew since the drivers had their bones picked clean by revelling raptors.

Darwin began to jog. He felt quite optimistic about finding Uncle Loops at first, but after he'd hurried along for almost half an hour, he still hadn't managed to catch up with him. He seemed to have vanished in the smog and as there was no smog Uptown, it could only mean one thing: Darwin was now Downtown – he had wandered into carnivore territory.

If he was honest, it was rather exciting. Darwin found Uptown a bit tame sometimes but this was a walk on the wild side. He'd never been to Raptor Road before and, not being exactly streetwise, he decided it wasn't nearly as dangerous as his parents led him to believe.

Darwin was mesmerised by the bright lights

and the strange smells and sounds. The place was buzzing – mainly due to the bluebottles swarming around the meat market which was still open for trade.

He hurried past the stalls, trying not to gag at the great carcasses of meat hanging up for sale. The sight of a whole plesiosaur garnished with seaweed made his guts churn. There were plenty of dodgy-looking customers wandering about

and the butchers – mostly burly baryonyx –
were shouting out their wares.

'Steggy sausages, get your luvverly steggy-
sausages here!'

'Mastodon mince! Fresh mastodon, killed
today!'

'Brachioburgers! Brontoburgers! Walk up,
walk up!'

They were doing a roaring trade. Darwin was

feeling a bit nervous now – all the meat came
from herbivores and he was worried he might
come across a long-lost relative among a tray of
chops. Uncle Loops might have been turned
into meat balls already.

'Can I help you, pal?' said the butcher who
owned the
burger stall.
Realising that
Darwin was not
one of them, he
lowered his
voice. 'Fancied a
bit of the red
stuff, did you? I've got a lovely bit of triceratop
toe – want me to put it in a brown bag so no
one will know?'

'No thanks,' quivered Darwin. 'You haven't seen
an old stegosaurus hanging around, have you?'

The butcher gazed up at the slabs of flesh dangling from their hooks and shook his head.

'No demand for old stegosaurus,' he said. 'Too tough. They make a tasty stew but they need a lot of slow cooking.'

Darwin swallowed hard. It was obvious that the carnivores thought all herbivores were dinnersaurs and as his fears for his uncle – and himself – grew, he broke into a run.

'Uncle Loops? Uncle Loops, where are you?' he called, blundering away from the stinking market stalls into a maze of pubs, clubs and seedy shops. It felt as if everyone was looking at him and licking their lips. He decided to go home – but which way was that? Darwin had taken so many twists and turns, he was completely lost.

Panicking, he ran blindly down an alley and as he paused for breath, he looked up and saw a familiar face.

'Ozzi!' He smiled.

The herbivores never usually smiled when they saw Ozzi but it was such a relief to see someone he knew, Darwin forgot about the square bike wheel and went to shake hands. The australopithecus seemed confused by Darwin's greeting, pulled his hairy paw away and set his cynognathus on him.

'Good Nogs,' said Darwin, trying to befriend the beast. 'No nipping.'

Ozzi barked at Nogs, who whimpered and scuttled back to him.

'Ozzi, have – you – seen – Uncle – Loops?' said Darwin slowly.

Nobody was quite sure how intelligent Ozzi was. He seemed unable to speak Dino but was known to grunt and do finger gestures.

'You know Uncle Loops,' Darwin reminded him, 'the old stegosaurus who lives with my family in Fossil Street?'

Ozzi nodded enthusiastically and pointed to the narrow entrance between The Prawn Shop and the funeral parlour.

'He went that way? You're not as stupid as they say, are you?' said Darwin kindly. 'Thank you, Ozzi. I'll never forget this.'

And he never did forget. It soon became clear Ozzi had sent him down a dark tunnel – straight into the path of an oncoming train.

Darwin's short little life flashed before him as he prepared to die, when suddenly somebody grabbed him and pulled him to safety. Darwin turned to thank his rescuer, but stopped in fright.

It was a velociraptor.

In a tight-fitting mini dress.

Who introduced herself as Liz Vicious.

She looked friendly.

'Isn't it past your bedtime, little veggie?' she said, blowing on her nails. 'Are you some kind of runaway? Believe me, these streets are not paved with Golden Delicious.'

'I'm lost,' said Darwin. 'Do you know the way to Fossil Street, please, Liz?'

'It's Miss Vicious to you,' she said, taking him

a little too firmly by the hand. As she led him back through the market, Darwin began to wonder if she knew the way to Fossil Street at all.

'Are you taking me home, Miss Vicious?'

She gave him a sly half-smile. 'Kinda.'

'Only my mother and father are expecting me.'

'Shame.'

Darwin's blood ran cold. Maybe she wasn't as friendly as she looked. Maybe she hadn't stopped him from being rail-kill out of kindness. Maybe she just didn't fancy meat paste and wanted to eat him whole. 'Let me go! I'll throw a tantrum. I'll make a scene.'

Liz Vicious tightened her grip. 'It's not safe for a sprout like you to be Downtown all alone. I'm taking you to a safe house for the night.'

Darwin relaxed. His hunch had been right. Not all carnivores were bad and he hadn't been to a sleepover for ages. 'Could I phone my parents and tell them where I am? Mum is such a fusspot.'

'Don't worry. We'll call them for you.'

We? There had been no mention of 'we' before. 'Who else is at the safe house?'

'You'll meet them soon enough,' said the raptor, stopping outside a rough-looking dive called The Prehysterical. There was a massive, bear-like bouncer on the door – a megatherium – who was sorting out a couple of rowdy raptors.

'I rent a room over the club,' said Liz. 'You can stay there. Don't worry about the punters. They get a bit crazy on a Saturday night . . . in you go, babe.'

She gave Darwin a shove. The dance hall was bumping. The music was so loud, he put his hands over his ears but it wasn't enough to block out the remarks from the assorted carnivores propping up the bar.

'Look at the meat on that!'

'Nice catch, Liz. Can we tear and share?'

'He'd go down nicely with a bit of Steggae Steggae Sauce!'

It was quieter out the back, but instead of heading upstairs, Liz Vicious took him down a flight of stairs to the basement and knocked on the door.

'Who is it? If it's the tax man, you can rock off. If it's the police, I ain't in.'

'It's me,' called Liz. 'I've brought you some supper.' She pushed Darwin through the door and there, sitting behind a table playing poker with a mean pteranadon and a muscle-bound deinosuchus was a nasty-looking tyrannosaurus wearing a solid gold watch. Darwin recognised it at once. It was no longer on a chain – its new owner had put a newt-skin strap on it and buckled it round his wrist.

Flint Beastwood put his cards down and looked at Darwin sideways. 'I don't remember

ordering any veg, Elizabeth.'

'Found him on the wrong side of the track,' said Liz, 'looking for his Uncle Poopy.'

'L-Loops,' stammered Darwin.

Flint Beastwood stroked the watch fondly. 'Loops? The same Loops who gave me this timepiece? Are you the nephew I met at the party? You herbivores all look the same to me. What's your name again?'

'Darwin.'

'Welcome to my humble abode,' said Flint. 'Let me fix you something to eat.'

'Good thinking, boss. Fatten him up,' squawked Terry O'Dactyl.

'I've seen more meat on a butcher's pencil,' grunted Mr Cretaceous.

Flint Beastwood held up a claw. 'Simmer down, lads. That's no way to speak to our guest. We must take care of him.'

He picked up the phone and dialled an extension number. 'Is that you Dippy Egg, you thick piece of toast? Move your bald butt and bring my little guest something nice to eat . . . now!'

Darwin's head was in a spin. Despite ruining

Uncle Loops's party and stealing his watch, the T. Rex seemed to quite like him. He decided the best thing to do was stay calm and polite. 'Mr Beastwood, please may I borrow your phone to call my parents?'

'Certainly,' said Flint. 'We want them to know exactly where you are, don't we? In fact, I'll do it myself. Gimme the number.'

Darwin watched as Beastwood dialled. Boy, am I in big trouble, he thought. My dad is going to kill me. He told me never to go Downtown and here I am, disobeying his orders.

'Ah, Mr Stigson,' said Flint. There was a long pause, then he continued. 'Yes, that's right, it's Mr Beastwood here. I have your son Darwin at my headquarters . . . Yes, I'm sure you told him not to come here, but . . . ha, ha . . . boys will be boys, Maurice.'

'Can I speak to Dad?' whispered Darwin.

'Maurice, he wants to say hello.' Beastwood held the mouthpiece to Darwin's lips.

'Hi, Dad,' squeaked Darwin. 'Sorry I didn't come straight home, I —'

Flint snatched the phone away and carried on talking to Mr Stigson. 'He'll be safe with me,' said Flint. 'He can go home as soon as you pay me the ransom — let's say a million, shall we? What? No, that's not just my little joke. I never joke about money, Maurice. I'm a carnivore.'

The tyrannosaurus put the receiver down carefully. 'Mr Cretaceous, would you and Terry kindly escort our young friend to the cellar. I've counted his limbs, so no nibbling. I need him in one piece.'

'Aw, boss,' sulked Terry O'Dactyl. 'Not even a tiny bite?'

'Not even a little toe. Why the long face, Darwin? Daddy loves you, doesn't he? He'll pay me the ransom and home you go, no harm done. Dippy will look after you.'

With that, Beastwood's henchmen bundled Darwin down another flight of stairs, threw him into a cold, damp room and tied him to a chair with a length of rope.

'We will leave you in the, um, care of Dippy Egg,' grunted Mr Cretaceous.

'He's demented, so he is! Doo-lally. Completely cuckoo,' tittered Terry O' Dactyl.

A skinny gallimimus sloped in, carrying a plate of green eyeballs in thick, red sauce. 'Couldn't get no stuffed olives,' he mumbled.

Suddenly, Darwin lost his appetite.

CHAPTER 5

BEEFCAKE

Meanwhile, back at Fossil Street, Uncle Loops had turned up shortly after Darwin went to look for him. Unfortunately, Mr Stigson assumed Darwin had gone by bike and would be too far away to catch up with, or he'd have run and told him that Loops had been found.

Mrs Stigson was the one to find Loops. She'd finished clearing up the mess the carnivores had made and, too tired to cook, she'd gone to the freezer to fetch a pizza and found the door open with Uncle Loops asleep on a mattress of frozen peas.

'Is it spring already?' he yawned as she shook him awake. 'Jurassic or Pliocene period?'

'What are you doing?' demanded Mrs Stigson. 'Darwin's out looking for you.'

'I am re-living the ice age,' explained Uncle Loops.

A few hours later, the dreaded phonecall had come from Flint Beastwood demanding the ransom. After a fitful night's sleep, the Stigsons were pulling their scales out trying to think of a way to get their son back. Even if they sold their house and every stick of furniture they still couldn't raise enough cash.

'If we don't come up with the money soon, Flint will have Darwin fossilised,' worried Mr Stigson. 'I'll have to swallow my pride and go cap in hand to the neighbours.'

Mrs Stigson picked up the phone. 'I'll ring round and ask them over. Hello, is that you, Phyllis? Would you like to come round for a coffee?'

'Will there be cake?' asked Mrs Merrick. 'I'm on my way.'

Within the hour, Sir Tempest Stratford, Frank, Ernest and the mayor had also agreed to come along.

'Where's young Darwin?' boomed Boris. 'I saw his bicycle in a bush. I see I'm not the only chap who's had his wheel changed – I expect it was that fuzzy, scuzzy Ozzi.'

'Darwin's been kidnapped.' Mrs Stigson wept into the sponge cake.

'Dry your eyes, Lydia. You'll dilute the jam,' said Mrs Merrick.

The herbivores were shocked and appalled when they heard about the ransom.

'We just don't have that kind of money,' admitted Mr Stigson. 'Any bright ideas?'

'How about a garage sale?' said Mrs Merrick.

'We haven't got a garage,' said Uncle Loops. 'You should sell the car, Maurice.'

'We don't have a car. We're trying to reduce our carbon footprint,' said Mr Stigson. 'Haven't you got anything stashed under your mattress, Augustus?'

'Yes!' said Uncle Loops. 'My spare false teeth.'

Once it was established that nobody in the room had any money – or at least none they were willing to part with – everyone turned to Boris for a brainwave.

'You're the mayor, dude,' said Frank and Ernest in unison. 'You didn't get where you are today by being a total waste of space.'

'Don't encourage him,' said Mrs Merrick. 'He'll want us all to "bond with the carnivores" in some silly sporting event or other . . .'

'Golf!' whooped Boris. 'We'll challenge Flint Beastwood to a game of golf and whoever wins gets to keep the kid.'

'Excuse me?' said Mr Stigson. 'You're playing for my son's life here.'

'Na-ha! But don't you see?' said Boris.

'There's no way Beastwood can beat me at golf. I've seen fish with longer arms. He couldn't swing a teaspoon, let alone a five iron.'

'We can't risk it,' said Mrs Stigson. 'He'll cheat. He'll find a way to beat you, probably with your own club. He's a carnivore, that's what they're like.'

Mr Stigson gazed out of the window thoughtfully. 'Lydia, that's just a stereotype. That's like saying all mastodons are greedy.'

'Why is everybody staring at me?' snapped Mrs Merrick with her mouth full of sponge. 'You should be thinking of ways of saving poor Darwin. You should never have let him go Downtown in the first place, Lydia. I wouldn't be seen dead there.'

'You would,' said Uncle Loops. 'Your great carcass could feed a family of velociraptors into the next millennium.'

'What's Ozzi doing out there, Maurice?' asked Mrs Stigson quickly.

Mr Stigson had been watching the australopithecus out of the window for some time. He appeared to have something to sell in an old wheelbarrow.

'Probably old wheels,' said Uncle Loops.

Mr Stigson banged on the window. 'Shoo! Be off with you.'

Ozzi ignored him and held up what appeared to be a chocolate cake the size of a dustbin lid.

Mrs Merrick's trunk began to water. 'Go and see what it is, Maurice. If it's black forest gateau, I'll have two.'

As Mr Stigson went off to see what the

australopithecus had on offer, Mrs Merrick spoke firmly to the remaining herbivores. 'If you lot had anything about you, you'd form a posse, march into Beastwood's headquarters and rescue Darwin before it's too late.'

'All for one and one for all!' chorused the twin ankylosaurs, duelling with rolled up newspapers.

'Count me in,' said Sir Tempest. 'I'm an accomplished swordsman, ask my agent. I had the leading role in *The Three Musky Deers*.' He grabbed the Sunday supplement and joined in.

'No, no. You can't expect to dispatch carnivores with a copy of the *Daily Wail*,' tutted Mrs Merrick. 'You'll have to fight properly – with horns and spikes.'

Frank and Ernest turned green.

'What . . . you mean kill them?' Frank said.

'Yes,' insisted Mrs Merrick. 'What were you going to do? Read them to death?'

'But that's cold-blooded murder,' said Frank earnestly. 'We're vegetarian pacifists.'

'And cowards,' said Ernest, frankly.

Sir Tempest Stratford dropped his paper sword. 'Blood makes me queasy,' he shuddered. 'We use ketchup on film shoots. I can't kill anyone for real, I'm an actor. It says so in my contract.'

'Sometimes,' said Mrs Merrick, 'I'm ashamed to be a herbivore . . . Ooh! Here's Maurice. What have you got there, one of Ozzi's cakes?'

Mr Stigson parked the wheelbarrow on the carpet. 'It's not for you,' he said brightly. 'It's luxury beefcake. I'm going to give it to Flint Beastwood instead of the ransom. I'm going to appeal to his better nature.'

'He hasn't got one,' said Mrs Merrick. 'He's a carnivore. Either you give him the money or you'll have to fight him tooth and claw. I never thought I'd hear myself saying this but for once, cake isn't the answer.'

'You're being rather pessimistic,' said Mr Stigson.

The phone rang. Uncle Loops got to it first. 'Not today, thank you. My nephew is being held to ransom, I haven't got time for chit chat, goodbye.' He slammed it back down.

'Who was that?' asked Mrs Stigson.

'Some fellow called Beastwood,' said Uncle Loops airily. 'No one we know.'

For a second, Mr Stigson forgot he was a peaceful herbivore and almost strangled him.

'That's the tyrannosaurus who kidnapped my son! You cut him off!'

The phone rang again.

'Want me to get that?' said Uncle Loops.

'Noooooo!' cried Mr Stigson, wrestling the phone off him. 'Give it to me, Loops. Ouch! Hello? Yes, I am he . . . Yes, I will . . .' He put the phone down. 'It was Beastwood. He wants me to meet him behind The Prehysterical with the money at midday. We'll just have to hope he likes luxury beefcake. Who's coming with me?'

The neighbours took a while to volunteer, but as Mrs Merrick scowled at them in turn, they slowly put their hands up.

'I will,' said Boris, 'if you all promise to vote for me next year.'

'I will, if you all promise not to,' said Mrs Merrick. 'Come along, you bunch of losers. You too, Sir Tempest.'

'I'll have to ask my —'

'If you say "agent" once more, I'm going to push your face in that beefcake,' said Mr Stigson. 'Are you coming, Lydia?'

Mrs Stigson shook her head. 'I'm going to see Lou Gooby. She's probably busy meditating, but I have to ask for her help.'

'What, that phoney old guru?' said Mr Stigson, somewhat offended. 'Well, thanks a lot but I'm perfectly capable of getting my own son back.'

As Mrs Stigson watched her husband march off with his luxury beefcake towards Downtown, followed by his band of gentle giants, she had a nasty feeling this was going to end in tears.

'Wait for me!' hollered Uncle Loops.

Now she was certain it would.

CHAPTER 6

EARTHQUAKE

'Darwin? Don't tell no one – I've got you some nice, hot swamp soup,' said Dippy Egg, slopping the green liquid over the side of the bowl.

Since the day before, the two of them had secretly become friends and as Darwin couldn't face the maggotty meat his carnivorous captors provided, Dippy had been sneaking him vegetarian snacks.

He had untied Darwin for the night so he could sleep more comfortably, but they had both stayed awake until dawn looking at books. Although he looked older, it turned out that the gentle gallimimus was the same age as Darwin and not nearly as daft as Beastwood said he was. True, he didn't know his alphabet but, as he told Darwin, he'd never been to school. He'd been adopted as an orphan by Liz Vicious and forced into slavery.

'Have a sip of my soup,' Darwin offered.

Dippy gulped it down. He liked the occasional beetle but he was mostly vegan and as the rancid meat scraps Beastwood threw him made him feel ill, he was half-starved. 'Thanks. I hate the boss's guts,' said Dippy.

'Can't you leave them on the side of the plate?' suggested Darwin.

Dippy shook his head. 'I've got to get out of here. I want to go to university and study quantum physics. Can you teach me to read some more, Darwin?' He held out the book he'd stolen from Flint's library and Darwin went over the basics.

'Let's run through the alphabet again shall we?' said Darwin. 'A is for . . . ?'

'Allosaur,' said Dippy, beaming.

'B is for . . .?'

'Brachiosaur! C is for ceratops, D is for deinosuchus . . .'

Dippy Egg was a very quick learner and by five minutes to midday, he was happily reading the sports pages in the *Daily Wail*. At four minutes to midday, he heard the heavy footsteps of Mr Cretaceous on the stairs and, panicking,

he quickly tied Darwin back up with the rope. 'You'll be all right. I bet your old man's brought the dosh,' he whispered, but Darwin wasn't convinced.

'Dad hasn't got that kind of money.'

Mr Cretaceous booted the door open and belched. 'Out the way, Dipstick. Let's be havin' you. Upsadaisy, Darwin.'

Lifting him chair and all onto one shoulder, the deinosuchus stomped back upstairs and carried Darwin out to the car park behind The Prehysterical where Beastwood was waiting with Terry O'Dactyl and Liz Vicious. The tyrannosaurus looked at his gold watch.

'Hmm. Mr Stigson is two minutes late. I'm not happy about that.'

'He's coming, boss. He's coming, look!' tittered Terry. 'He's brought half of Fossil Street with him, so he has. Cor, they don't half look juicy!'

Mr Stigson appeared from around the corner with the neighbours in tow, pushing a wheelbarrow covered with a tea towel. Darwin's heart leapt. It must be full of notes.

'Ah, Mr Stigson,' said Beastwood, 'I've been expecting you.'

Mr Stigson gave him a friendly smile. 'Hello, Flint. Sorry we're late. Mrs Merrick needed the loo and then Sir Tempest lost his contact lens but here we all are.'

The tyrannosaurus glared at him. 'Cut the small talk, Maurice. What's in the wheelbarrow? It had better be money.'

'Ah, well, I thought about it,' said Mr Stigson, 'but then I thought, money's the easy option. What would Flint *really* like? So I got you this instead.'

He whipped the tea towel off and showed him the cake. 'It's beef.'

The tyrannosaurus flexed his hand and out

popped his killer claw like a giant pen knife.

'It's luxury,' said Mr Stigson as the neighbours tiptoed backwards.

'We thought you'd like that and a jolly old game of golf,' added Boris.

'Golf,' said Beastwood, stroking his chin. 'You thought I'd like that, did you?' His eyes glittered darkly.

Terry O'Dactyl hid his head under his skinny wings and folded up like a ghastly umbrella.

'It had better be very good beefcake,' snarled Beastwood.

As he opened his massive jaws and took a great bite, Darwin shrank into the chair. For a moment, the boss chewed thoughtfully, then with a thunderous snort of disgust he gagged and spat it out in a great sticky lump which landed on Mr Stigson's shoe.

'It's sprouts!' he screeched, stamping and

spitting like a toddler. 'Ugh. Eugh . . . I have to kill you. You tried to poison me.'

'I didn't,' protested Mr Stigson. 'I bought that cake in good faith from the australopithecus. He told me it was one hundred per cent meat and suitable for carnivores. He set me up!'

Beastwood lurched towards him gnashing his razor sharp teeth. If Dippy hadn't stuck his foot out and tripped him up, Mr Stigson would have got his head ripped off. As it was, the tyrannosaurus fell in an undignified heap. Mrs Merrick seized the opportunity, and sat on him.

Spotting the gold watch, Uncle Loops bent down and undid the buckle. 'Nice compass. I had one just like it. Pity this ladies' strap won't fit my wrist.'

Flint snatched the watch back as Mr Cretaceous levered the massive mastodon off his boss.

'Quick, untie me, Dippy,' hissed Darwin as the ankylosaurs ran around whacking O'Dactyl on the backside with newspapers. 'I need to rescue my uncle.'

While Dippy released Darwin, the other

herbivores were joining in the fight. 'Let's sneak up on that deinosuchus, Sir Tempest!' said Boris gallantly. 'I'll grab his tail, you slap his face.'

Sir Tempest put his snout in the air. 'No, I only act fights. I'm not doing it without a stunt man.'

'You're the limit, Stratford!' said Boris, grabbing the wheelbarrow and running it over Mr Cretaceous's foot. The deinosuchus hopped about sobbing like a baby.

'Crocodile tears,' sung Sir Tempest. 'That's very poor acting, I must say.'

'No one likes a critic!' cackled Liz Vicious, jumping onto his back and tearing his bowtie with her claws.

By now, Darwin was running over to Uncle Loops, who was busy trying to get his 'compass' back. Beastwood was stalking towards Loops and no matter how hard Darwin kicked Flint, he wouldn't back off.

'Dad, do something!' Darwin yelled. 'Flint's about to eat Uncle Loops!'

As Flint opened his mouth just wide enough to bite Uncle Loops's skull, the ground began to shake. His jaw froze, and as Uncle Loops's head lay on the tyrannosaurus's tongue, the rest of the carnivores stopped mid-fight and looked around anxiously.

The ground shook harder. Trees trembled and buildings began to buckle. The earth was bouncing them up and down like a trampoline and as the deafening *thump*, *thump*, *thump* got louder, there could be only one explanation.

'Earthquake!' shrieked Terry O'Dactyl.

The carnivores ran round in circles, snapping at each other in their frenzy. Unlike the herbivores, they didn't know the real cause of the shaking. As the sun was blocked out by the mighty frame of a mamenchisaurus, the

carnivores fell to their knees.

'Lou Gooby,' sighed Mr Stigson, spotting his wife walking behind her. 'There was no need, I had everything under control, Lydia.'

'Good show, Lou-Lou,' said Boris. 'Come to sort these scoundrels out? That's the way.'

The mamenchisaurus stood, as imposing as a mountain, and spoke. She was quite docile but the carnivores didn't know that and were spooked by her Chinese accent and soft, calm tone. 'Fighting between species is not answer. It only lead to extinction.'

'At one hundred and ninety, I'm nearly extinct already,' yelled Uncle Loops.

Darwin shushed him as Lou Gooby continued.

'No more fighting. You must channel brute force and stamina through sport.'

The carnivores tutted under their breath and even Boris looked slightly peeved.

'That was my idea. I've been saying that for

ages,' he muttered to anyone who would listen. 'Didn't I say cricket? Didn't I say golf?'

Lou stamped her foot and they all fell silent. Even though the herbivores knew she was a

gentle tree-grazer, they were in awe of her. She
was the closest thing they had to religion – they
believed in Gooby and with her head touching
the heavens, she commanded
huge respect.

'You will hold great
sporting event. You will call
it Dinosaur Olympics.'

'My idea,' grumbled
Boris.

'It will be held in
No Man's Land,' said Lou.
'Team Carnivore versus Team Herbivore. Mayor
will be judge.'

'That's me!' said Boris, perking up. 'Goody.
Can I have a stopwatch?'

The mamenchisaurus lowered her neck
which was the length of a big dipper and
nodded towards Uncle Loops's watch which

was strapped again to Flint's puny wrist. 'This will be ceremonial stopwatch of Dinosaur Olympics.'

Beastwood undid the watch stroppily and drew back as she picked it up in her tombstone teeth and gave it to Boris.

'What's in it for the winners?' asked Mr Cretaceous. 'Do we get to hit the losers?'

'Honourable winner get gold medal,' explained Lou Gooby. 'Team who win most gold medal get to take home Olympic torch.'

The carnivores talked amongst themselves, convinced they would knock seven bells out of the herbivores in every event and romp home to victory.

'All right then, you're on!" said Flint.

The carnivores were getting cocky now and began to chant at the herbivores like rowdy football fans.

'You're gonna get your freaky heads kicked in, oh yeah, oh yeah.'

'One T. O'Dactyl, there's only one T. O'Dactyl – one T. O'Dactyl!'

Lou Gooby put her foot down again which started an avalanche somewhere north of the equator and the raucous singing petered out to a muffled whimper. 'There will be strict rule,' she said. 'Anyone eat other competitor? Disqualify!'

Flint pulled a pained expression. 'As if we'd do a thing like that. Let's grab that torch, shall we lads?'

'Rule of entry,' said Lou, fixing him with her fathomless eyes, 'competitor can not enter Dinosaur Olympics if guilty of kidnap.'

'Me?' said the tyrannosaurus. 'Kidnap? Perish the thought, that's not in my nature.'

'You kidnapped my boy and demanded a ransom,' said Mr Stigson, hiding behind his wife.

Flint Beastwood shook his head. 'I've a good mind to call my lawyer. I rescued Darwin from the streets and put him up for the night like a kindly uncle. Held him to ransom, Maurice? Never.'

'You phoned me up and demanded a large sum of money,' retorted Mr Stigson.

Flint threw up his hands in fake bewilderment. 'Why would you think that unless . . . Ah! I know who's behind this: the australopithecus! He's an excellent mimic, he must have called you and pretended to be me. Have you heard his impression of me? It's scarily life-like, ask anyone.'

'It's not impossible, Maurice,' said Boris. 'Just because we've never heard him speak doesn't mean that he can't.'

'He's capable of anything,' trumpeted Mrs Merrick. 'Look how he tricked you with the cake. Is there any left, by the way?'

'The little scallywag,' said Mr Stigson. 'I owe you an apology, Mr Beastwood.'

He held out his hand for the tyrannosaurus to shake.

'Don't listen to him, Dad!' said Darwin. 'He's lying.'

His father winced as Beastwood held his hand in a vice-like grip.

'My, that's a firm handshake, Flint. I'll deal with you when we get home, Darwin.'

'Good luck in Olympics,' said Lou Gooby as she drifted off home. 'May best team win!'

But what were the chances of that happening?

CHAPTER 7

IN AT THE DEEP END

As Darwin helped Uncle Loops into his trunks in the swimming pool changing rooms, he was beginning to regret entering the Dinosaur Olympics. The categories had recently been announced by Lou Gooby and all the herbivores had been told to enter, regardless of their age, skill or fitness level.

It was Boris's fault. Being made judge had gone to his rather large head and he insisted that everybody went in for as many events as possible, though how Mrs Merrick was going to cope with the high jump was anybody's guess.

'Mastodons don't jump,' she told Boris. 'We haven't got the knees for it.'

'I don't want to hear any lame excuses,' blustered Boris. 'It's all about having the right mental attitude.'

'I have high hopes for the one hundred metres,' said Uncle Loops as a snail overtook him.

'You'll be fine,' insisted Boris. 'You just need to train. Phyllis, since you are not a dinosaur, perhaps you can be our coach instead. I want you to knock this lot into shape.'

'I'll knock you out of shape in a minute,' muttered Mrs Merrick. 'Besides, not all the carnivores are dinosaurs, either.'

'I think if anyone points it out to them, they won't be pointing to anything else again,' Boris told her.

Even Mr Stigson, who was usually a good sport, had his doubts that they could win the Olympics no matter how hard they tried. 'I'm game for anything,' he said. 'But us beat the carnivores? It's a tad unrealistic.'

Boris gave a long blast on his ref's whistle until he went red in the face 'It isn't open for discussion! Lou Gooby has spoken. Now drag your lazy bones down to the swimming pool. I expect great things from you in the diving event.'

While most of the herbivores weren't keen on being made to exercise, Darwin was really enjoying it. He was confident that he could win several events, including the pole vault. His parents would be so proud of him and, thrilled at the prospect of being a sporting hero, he whistled merrily as he slipped into his swimming shorts.

It was only when he pulled them up that the whistling stopped. Somehow, they'd grown far too big for him – he could now get his whole body through one of the legs. Either he'd shrunk or his shorts had grown.

'Uncle Loops?' he called. 'Have you got my swimming stuff?'

There was a short pause.

'Only if there's something you're not telling me,' said the voice in the next cubicle.

Darwin put a towel round himself and whipped back the curtain.

'I just found these in my cubicle and thought I'd try them on,' explained Uncle Loops. 'They're rather comfy.' He was now wearing enormous, pink, bikini bottoms with big frills.

'Who's stolen my cozzie?' bellowed Mrs Merrick. 'Was it you, Sir Tempest? I know you dress-up for a living but this is going too far!'

Sir Tempest strode out of his changing room wearing a skimpy pair of swimming shorts. 'I don't think these are yours, Phyllis. They'd be a bit snug. Do they belong to you perhaps, Mrs Stigson?'

'They're mine,' said Mr Stigson, sticking his head out from behind a changing curtain. 'I can't even get into these!'

'Those are ours,' confessed Frank and Ernest who had the great misfortune of having their swimming trunks replaced by Uncle Loops's long-johns and were in a leg each.

 'You know who's behind is behind this, don't you?' said Darwin, who'd discovered something very unsavoury in an empty cubicle. He held up a pair of tiny Y-fronts.

'Why don't they have a tail hole at the back?' asked Mrs Stigson.

'Whoever these belong to doesn't have a tail,' said Darwin.

'Whoever it is, their fashion sense is appalling,' said Sir Tempest, smirking. 'I wouldn't wish those on my worst enemy.'

'I've a nasty feeling they *do* belong to our worst enemy,' sighed Darwin.

The herbivores groaned in unison. The australopithecus had been at it again!

'The little monster has been in here and swapped our swimming costumes around!' gasped Mrs Merrick. 'If his briefs are here, whose bathers is he running round in?'

'Oh no,' said Mrs Stigson under her breath. She had visions of Ozzi skipping down Fossil Street in her itsy-bitsy floral bikini and wished to goodness she'd worn something sensible.

Embarrassed, they exchanged their swimming costumes, with Mrs Stigson being excused.

Only Uncle Loops was disappointed. 'I liked that pink swimsuit,' he sulked. 'I get bunched up in long-johns.'

'Why are you all standing at the shallow end?' Mrs Merrick barked when everyone was finally ready. 'The deep end is over there, it says so clearly on that sign. Make your way swiftly to the edge and dive in . . . No, not with your zimmer frame, Uncle Loops.'

The herbivores lined up in a miserable row.

Darwin stared into the water and lifted up his goggles in alarm. 'Mrs Merrick? I'd be a lot happier diving down the other end.'

'Don't be a baby, Darwin,' snapped Mrs Merrick. 'It's not *that* deep.'

Darwin pointed to the pool frantically. 'I know it's not, that's why I . . .'

'I haven't got time for back-chat,' snapped Mrs Merrick, adjusting her bikini bottoms. 'Everybody ready? Pull your trunks up, Augustus. One, two, three, dive!'

There were a series of loud splashes followed by terrible moans and groans as the dinosaurs bruised their feet, shattered their kneecaps and bashed their heads on the bottom of the pool. The water was very shallow.

'I've got brain damage!' wailed Sir Tempest.

'Welcome to my world,' spluttered Uncle Loops.

'Someone must have meddled with the signs,' said Mr Stigson. 'Who would have done a stupid, dangerous thing like that?'

It was Darwin who noticed the trail of muddy, five-toed footprints leading from the changing rooms to the steps. Whoever the mysterious mammal was, it walked on two short legs. 'The australopithecus!' he announced.

As it turned out, Ozzi wasn't the only one who had sneaked into the pool to cause mayhem that morning. As the herbivores tried to perfect their diving techniques in the deep end, someone as well as Mrs Merrick was keeping a critical eye on them.

'That brat Darwin is the one to watch,' whispered Liz Vicious from behind a pillar. 'The others couldn't dive into a bar, but he's just pulled off a pike with a triple somersault.'

Terry O'Dactyl licked his pencil and scribbled madly into a notebook. 'So he's the one we have to knobble if we want to win the gold,' he tittered. 'On the big day, I'll sneak up and tie rocks to his ankles, so I will. Or just grab them and pull him under till he's drownded – woo hoo!'

'You're sick, Terry,' said the raptor, 'and I mean that in a good way. Beastie will be thrilled with the information we're gathering for him.'

They continued to watch for a while, jotting down the strengths and weaknesses of each competitor, all the better to cheat and beat them on the day. Finally, Mrs Merrick stopped the session and as the herbivores made their weary way back to the changing room, Beastwood's stooges left through the back door and hid in the gym.

❧　　❧　　❧

By the afternoon, Mrs Merrick decided to take the coaching seriously and split the team up.

'I want half of you to go to the gym to do

weight-lifting and boxing. The rest, find an open space in the park and practise running, jumping, vaulting and throwing the javelin.'

Sir Tempest folded his arms and huffed. 'I'm not running and jumping. Not after my operation.'

'The operation was on your nose, Stratford,' said Mr Stigson. 'You don't need your nose for those events.'

Mrs Merrick sighed. Coaching was very hungry work. She just wanted to go home, put her feet up and eat a fruit pie the size of a boulder. 'Sir Tempest, stop arguing. If you really don't feel like running and jumping, you can at least put the shot.'

'Certainly, Phyllis,' he said. 'Where would you like me to put it?'

Mrs Merrick gave him a withering look.

'Come along, Uncle Loops,' said Darwin. 'I'll

walk with you to the playing fields. You might not take the gold in the sprinting events but you'll be brilliant at the marathon.'

'Slow and steady, that's me,' said Uncle Loops, pottering off with his zimmer frame.

As the herbivores went their separate ways to practice, the cunningly camouflaged carnivores continued to take notes about their rivals' performance.

Having watched Mr Stigson dancing about

in the boxing ring, they decided he was no threat to Mr Cretaceous who could probably knock him out with his little finger. 'Those ankylosaur twins are pretty good though,' hissed Terry. 'Their tails could give Mr C a nasty headache.'

'There must be a way to handicap them,' whispered Liz. 'I'm sure Beastie will think of one.'

'He's really good at handicapping,' agreed O'Dactyl, scribbling down some gruesome suggestions of his own. Satisfied that they'd got the low-down on the herbivores at the gym, they sneaked off to the park to see just how useless the other competitors were.

They arrived just in time to see Sir Tempest drop the shot put on his foot. It was quite plain to Darwin that he'd done it on purpose. As the triceratops rolled about on the floor screaming, he managed to convince Mrs Merrick that he'd broken all his toes and she let him go and play on the swings.

A grisly smile spread over Liz's fangs. 'I think we've got this event well and truly in the bag, Terry.'

'Useless bunch of fossils,' he agreed. 'I can't wait to report back to the boss.'

And, as Mrs Stigson almost skewered Mrs Merrick like a kebab with a wayward javelin, that's exactly what they did.

CHAPTER 8

DIRTY TRICKS

'I can't believe it's the day of the Dinosaur Olympics already,' said Darwin as he ate a hearty breakfast.

'Wait till you get to my age,' said Uncle Loops. 'The days pass like minutes, the years pass like days. Only last week, it was the Meiocene Period, now here we are in . . . Heck, which century is it? They didn't have centuries when I was a kid.'

He watched Mr Stigson practising his jabs in the garden and twisted his finger in his ear as if he had a screw loose.

'I worry about your father, Darwin. Whoever it is he's trying to punch, they've gone.'

'He's shadow boxing,' explained Darwin. 'He's competing against Mr Cretaceous in the boxing event and he's determined to win.'

The phone rang and, fighting his uncle for the receiver, Darwin took the call.

'Hello? Can you speak up, please? I can hardly

hear what you're saying . . . Dippy, is that you?'

He stood and listened, his eyes swivelling in outrage. 'Flint Beastwood is going to do *what*? To *whom*? But that's cheating! Thanks for letting me know, Dippy.'

He put the phone down in disbelief. 'The carnivores have been spying on us while we were training,' he exclaimed. 'They're going to try and nobble any herbivore that might beat them!'

'Just you then,' said Uncle Loops.

Darwin shook his head. 'No, Frank and Ernest stand a great chance in the boxing, Mum is a surprisingly good shot-putter, and Sir Tempest throws the javelin well – he had professional training for a movie.'

Mr Stigson kept ducking and diving. 'We'd better get a move on,' he said. 'I'd hate to miss the opening ceremony. Apparently there's a firework display. Boris wheedled some funds out of the council. It was put aside for single mothers but he's used it to buy a bumper box of rockets.'

Slipping into their sports kits, the Stigsons hurried off to No Man's Land where the event was due to take place, armed with wire snippers and glue remover to combat any foul play. On the way, they met the rest of Team Herbivore and warned them about the dirty tactics the carnivores were going to use against them in the games.

'The swines,' wailed Sir Tempest.

'They don't know any better,' said Mr Stigson generously. 'Don't let your guard drop but *no* cheating, Team Herbivore. We're going to win this fair and square, everyone agreed?'

'Maurice, you're no fun,' tutted Uncle Loops as he slopped along in his trainers. 'Why have my slippers got laces?'

If the herbivores hoped to be the first ones at the stadium, they were disappointed. Team

Carnivore had already arrived, no doubt to tinker with the equipment. Looking smug, they were now dipping into Boris's box of fireworks, letting off jumping jacks and helping themselves to sparklers.

'Here come Team Herbivore. We're all here,' shouted Boris, punctuated by heart-stopping bangs and the smell of gunpowder. 'Let the opening ceremony begin.'

He lit the Olympic torch with great solemnity and held it up.

'Would you kindly make a speech, Sir Tempest, what with you being an —'

'Athlete!' insisted Sir Tempest, finishing Boris's sentence. 'I can't give a speech now, I'm getting into my role as an Olympian. If you're that desperate, call my agent. She knows the president of America. He's not in my league but he's cheap.'

Flint Beastwood made his way over to the Olympic torch. Flanked by Mr Cretaceous and Terry O'Dactyl, he whipped out his sparkler and held it in the flame.

'There's no need for a speech, eh lads?' he sneered. 'I can sum up the spirit of the Dinosaur Olympics in three little words.'

Flint's sparkler caught light and having made

sure there was no sign of a mamenchisaurus, he used it to write big, sparkly letters that lingered against the dull grey sky:

FOSSIL STREET LOSERS

'We'll see about that,' said Mr Stigson indignantly.

Mr Cretaceous made a rude gesture with a claw as the carnivores turned tail and made their way over to the events.

'May I remind you all of the rules?' boomed Boris as the herbivores tried to jostle to the front. 'I say! Order! Honestly, this is worse than the House of Commons. Oh, please yourselves. Let the fun and games begin.'

There was already a commotion going on down by the cricket nets where the shot put was taking place. Mr Cretaceous insisted that Mrs Stigson went first, but it was hardly out of politeness. Knowing that her rock had been tampered with, he was so certain her throw would come to a sticky end, he didn't even bother to watch and swaggered about, flexing his biceps.

'You ought to warm up,' suggested Mrs Merrick. 'I'd hate you to pull a muscle.'

'No point, luv, I'm cold-blooded,' grinned Mr Cretaceous.

Mrs Stigson shrugged, tucked the rock under her chin, whirled round like a tank on a skid pan, and threw it as if it was no heavier than a cupcake.

It whistled  across the park, landed with a thump in the pansy bed and embedded itself in the mud.

Mr Cretaceous dropped his great snappy jaws open in dismay.

'Good shot, Lydia,' said Sir Tempest. 'I expect you've had lots of practice hurling the crockery about indoors. I can't see anyone beating that throw, not even that muscley deinosuchus.'

Flint Beastwood was watching the event unfold with increasing annoyance. He'd strictly instructed Dippy to roll Mrs Stigson's rock in superglue and watched him carry out the order with his own eyes. How had the rock and the plan come unstuck?

'Maybe it was weak glue, Beastie,' cawed Liz Vicious.

But she was wrong. Mr Cretaceous picked up his shot, spun round in a circle and with a deafening grunt, he let go . . . At least, he tried to, but the rock stuck firmly to his hand and he took off with the put.

'It's your own fault for taking your eye off the ball,' said Mrs Stigson, who'd carefully swapped hers for his while he was busy admiring his own biceps.

Things weren't going smoothly at the long jump either. Uncle Loops had been the first to take part. He'd taken a run-up of 0.2 miles an hour, stepped into the sandpit, and trod in something smelly.

'It wasn't me that time,' he said, as Darwin scraped the stinking muck off Uncle Loops's trainers with a stick. 'I was scared but not that scared.'

'What a dirty trick,' said Mr Stigson. 'I didn't think Team Carnivore would poop so low.'

Mrs Merrick wrinkled her trunk. 'This isn't carnivore doings, Maurice. I recognise that smell.'

'It's Nog squit,' groaned Darwin.

It seemed that Ozzi's pet cynognathus had been using the long jump pit as a litter tray and, by the look of the sloppy brown piles in the sand, it had a stomach upset.

Since nobody fancied having to spend the rest of the day washing, it was generally agreed that the best thing to do was to cancel the long jump.

Darwin didn't mind; he trotted off to the swimming pool and was looking forward to the diving. Liz had done a pretty good half pike with a twist, and now it was Darwin's turn. Despite several attempts by Terry O'Dactyl to sneak stones down his trunks, he did a spectacular dive and Boris was the first to congratulate him.

'Well done, lad. The gold medal for diving goes to Team Herbivore!'

Flint Beastwood wasn't happy. 'Terry, you muppet! If you'd done what I asked, that little sprout would have drowned and Liz would have romped home in first place.'

'I couldn't push the pebbles down his shorts,' wheedled O'Dactyl. 'He'd got a stone-proof belt around them.'

Dippy winked at Darwin behind his boss's back as the two teams made their way over to the running track for the one hundred metre sprint. Thanks to him, the herbivores were well aware that their running lanes had been littered with drawing pins and mousetraps to slow them down. Having also been tipped off that their starting lines had been rubbed with lard, Mrs Merrick had sneaked out during the diving event to clean up the track beforehand. Even though the carnivores still won, at least it had been a fair race.

As the day went on, the tricks played by the carnivores from Raptor Road got worse, but, thanks to Dippy, the herbivores spotted them all.

Even so, it was hard to separate the genuine accidents from the murder attempts.

During the pole vault, nobody was quite sure whether the pole had been sawn through or if Sir Tempest's weight had snapped it in half like a bread stick.

It was perfectly clear who'd tried to ruin the javelin though. There was a big fuss when Mrs Stigson accidentally speared Liz's handbag with her last throw, but this was nothing compared to what happened shortly after.

Sir Tempest had just had his turn and, having hurtled his third javelin right over a distant hedge, Flint Beastwood had a lot to live up to. With a determined look on his face, he sprinted up to his mark. With all the strength his tiny arm could muster, the T. Rex lobbed his javelin into the air and, blown by the wind, it disappeared in the same direction over the hedge.

Flint rubbed his hands with glee, did a victory dance, then shrieked as a hail of tiny arrows came flying over the hedge like a swarm of angry wasps and stuck in his buttocks. He clutched himself in pain and glared at the herbivores.

'Which of you toe-rags hired a hit man?' he bellowed.

Judging by their faces, they were as mystified as he was.

'He's behind you!' said Mr Stigson.

Beastwood spun round just in time to see a small hairy head duck down behind the hedge. 'The australopithecus!' he roared. 'You monkey!'

'He probably thought he was under attack. Shall I get those little stingers out with my tweezers for you?' asked Mrs Merrick.

Grudgingly, the tyrannosaurus bent over and, as she performed this rather delicate operation,

Boris pedalled over with news of the scores so far.

'Nice to see you all bonding,' he boomed. 'The good news is that it's almost even-stevens on medals. Team Herbivore are only one medal behind Team Carnivore.'

'Don't talk to me about behinds,' winced Flint.

'I can't believe we're not in the lead,' tutted Darwin.

Mr Stigson frowned. 'That's not very sporting, son. It's the taking part that counts.'

'Is it phooey!' said Uncle Loops indignantly. 'The ref's a ninny. I demand a recount.'

Boris double-checked the results on his clipboard. 'Let me see . . . no, I'm not a ninny. Despite Frank and Ernest's best efforts, Mr Cretaceous took the gold for the boxing, but you can catch up if you win the high jump.'

'You'll have a job beating Dippy Egg,' snorted Flint. 'That great long streak has legs like spaghetti.'

Darwin looked at his own stumpy legs. Jumping wasn't one of his strengths but if he ran fast enough and bounced high enough, maybe he could win.

'That's the spirit,' said Mr Stigson as they went over to the high jump arena. 'Keep your chin up and stay focused.'

A crowd had already gathered and, as Boris set the bar, Darwin limbered up, stretching his calves. He was first to jump. After a couple of knee-bends, he took a swerving run-up, leapt and to his amazement, he cleared the bar by a centimetre.

Mrs Stigson wasn't quite so lucky. Unable to get much lift, she sat on the bar and bent it into a loop, and Frank and Ernest had to hammer it straight with their clubbed tails. When it was their turn, both ankylosaurs hit the bar and when it was replaced, Uncle Loops – the last herbivore to compete – made no attempt to jump at all and walked under it.

It was Team Carnivore's turn. If Liz Vicious hadn't insisted on carrying her handbag, doubtless she'd have taken silver. Mr Cretaceous attempted to fling himself over backwards and got his toes in a tangle and Terry O'Dactyl was disqualified for cheating even though he missed the bar by a hundred metres.

'Out!' said Boris as the pteranodon landed. 'You're not allowed to fly over it.'

'Boo!' hooted the carnivores. 'Not fair!'

'That's rich coming from you,' snapped Mrs Merrick.

Dippy Egg, just as everyone predicted, jumped with ridiculous ease, leaving only himself and Darwin in the competition. A hush fell as Boris raised the bar. Darwin gulped. He didn't stand a chance.

'Go on, Darwin, we're rooting for you, son,' said Mr Stigson.

Darwin skipped on the spot for a few seconds, took a deep breath, ran at the bar and, at the very last second, tucked his knees under his chin and waited for the dreaded sound of the bar clattering to the ground. It never came. He'd just managed to skim it – but as he lay upside down in the sandpit, he could see it wobbling. Please don't fall, please don't fall, he prayed, and despite Mr Cretaceous blowing as hard as he could, the bar stayed put. A cheer went up from the herbivores – but it wasn't over yet.

It was Dippy's turn. He lollopped towards the posts but as he went to jump, he skidded on something, his legs flew up in the air and the bar crashed down on his head.

Team Carnivore let out a team groan.

'You clumsy duck!' yelled Beastwood as Dippy staggered dizzily back to his team.

'Sorry, boss. The marble you gave me to knobble the veggies fell out of my pocket.'

Mrs Stigson ran over to congratulate her boy. 'Darling, you won!' she exclaimed, smothering Darwin in kisses.

He fought her off and looked embarrassed. It wasn't the kisses so much, but he suspected that Dippy had let him win. While he was happy for his team to have another medal, he felt he couldn't really take the credit for his achievement.

Boris walked over and patted him on the back. 'Congratulations. That's another gold for Team Herbivore. Which means we have a tie! Whoever wins the final event of the day wins the Dinosaur Olympics.'

The cross-country marathon was the herbivores' last chance.

CHAPTER 9

SINK OR SWIM

While both teams had tried to enter their best athletes for the other events, everyone had to take part in the marathon, no matter how useless they were. The idea was to go out of the park, run three times round the primeval forest, then back to the finishing line by the monkey bars in the playground. It was twenty-five kilometres in all and when Uncle Loops found out, he rummaged around in his pockets for his bus pass.

'I can't walk all that way,' he protested. 'Not after the day I've had.'

'You can do it, Uncle,' said Darwin as the contestants took their positions on the starting line. 'Just walk slowly if you want.'

'Like I have an option,' muttered the old stegosaurus.

'I'm gonna have you, Grandad,' said Mr Cretaceous, who was in the next lane.

Uncle Loops gave him an old-fashioned look. 'Oh yeah? Eat my long-johns.'

Boris waved his starter gun. 'Now, now. Let's be nice to each other. No pushing, no cheating, no eye-gouging.'

He held up Uncle Loops's birthday watch and waited for the big hand to reach the twelve. 'On your marks, get set . . .'

BANG!!

They were off, with Darwin in the lead, but to everyone's annoyance, Boris called them back.

'False start! Back to the starting line. You too, Mr Beastwood.'

Mrs Merrick was particularly annoyed. It was almost teatime and she was anxious for the games to finish so she didn't miss her afternoon cakes.

Boris looked at his gun in disbelief. 'Hmm . . . I didn't pull the trigger. It wasn't my gun that went off.'

There was another series of bangs and a rocket zipped through Mr Cretaceous's hat and left a little smouldering hole.

Team Herbivore followed the smoke trail of the rocket to the top of the fun slide and there was the australopithecus moving the Olympic torch too close to the closing ceremony fireworks.

'Shoo!' said Mrs Merrick, charging over to the playground. 'You're pathetic!'

'Don't be too harsh on him, Phyllis,' said Mr

Stigson. 'We've clearly frightened him. It's just a feeble attempt to scare us off. After all, we are on his territory – this is No Man's Land and he's no man.'

Sir Tempest wasn't in the mood to be politically correct. 'You'll be putting food out for him next, Maurice. He's not a cute little hapalops, he's really quite evolved and . . . Good grief, is he wearing a bikini?'

Mrs Stigson recognised it immediately and changed the subject. 'He's just attention-seeking. Don't look at him – that's what he wants. He's going now, so let's get on with the marathon, shall we?'

As Ozzi scuttled away with Nogs, everyone got back on their marks.

'Get set . . .' said Boris.

BANG!!

They were off again with Darwin in the lead for a second time, closely followed by Liz Vicious.

'Stop!' yelled Boris. 'False start! It still wasn't my gun.'

'You're having a larf,' grumped Mr Cretaceous, pushing his snout into Boris's. 'It can't be Ozzi, he's run off.'

Boris was just about to be dismembered when Uncle Loops stood up and made a confession. 'It was me who went bang.' He held up a party popper. 'I found it in my pocket, pulled the string and it just went off in my hand.'

The dinosaurs glared at him.

'What?' said Uncle Loops. 'It was left over from my birthday party.'

By now, even mild-mannered Boris was getting impatient. 'Well, if you want to have another one, I suggest you be quiet and let me start the race.'

It was third time lucky. As the starter gun went off, the marathon began and although Darwin was in front at first, by the time they got out of the park, the carnivores had streaked ahead.

'Pace yourselves,' said Mr Stigson. 'They may be faster than us, but they don't have our stamina.'

'That might be true,' harrumphed Mrs

Merrick, who was running alongside them in support, 'but has anybody thought to bring any doughnuts? I shall fade away if I don't eat soon.'

Nobody had, but as they entered the forest they were heartened to see Flint Beastwood clutching a stitch in his side and Mr Cretaceous sitting on a log, wheezing. Darwin was all for breaking into a sprint and overtaking them but Mr Stigson didn't agree.

'You don't want to exhaust yourself. Keep

going steady and, one by one, the carnivores will wear themselves out.'

'Listen to you, Maurice,' said Mrs Merrick. 'I thought I was the coach.'

'You are, you're the slow coach,' said Uncle Loops as they stopped in a clearing. 'I wish I had my compass. Which way are we meant to go now?'

'Put your glasses on,' snapped Sir Tempest. 'There's a signpost over there. I suggest we go in the direction in which it's pointing unless you have a better idea.'

'I don't have any idea,' shrugged Uncle Loops. 'I'm one hundred and ninety-nine.'

'One hundred and ninety,' Darwin reminded him as they all trotted after Sir Tempest.

Uncle Loops did the maths and with a huge smile, he speeded up. 'One hundred and ninety you say? Suddenly I feel nine years younger!'

After an hour of following signposts, they seemed to be going deeper and deeper into the forest. It was impossible to run any more because the path was blocked by thick brambles and Team Herbivore and Team Carnivore found themselves herded together in a clump.

'This doesn't feel right, boss,' said Terry O'Dactyl, who was having a panic attack.

'Stop your flapping and breathe,' said Mrs Merrick. 'You're making me jittery. Now, where are we, Maurice?'

Mr Stigson prided himself on his navigation skills and refused to admit defeat. 'Don't worry, I know exactly where we are, folks.'

'So do I,' said Uncle Loops. 'Lost.'

'Nonsense,' said Mr Stigson, battling his way through the undergrowth. 'There's a chalk arrow on that tree trunk. We must head east. Follow me!'

'He's a marvel,' simpered Sir Tempest. 'Come along, Mr Beastwood, you must admit that Maurice is a marvel. I'm waiting . . .'

Mr Beastwood admitted nothing of the sort. After another hour of blundering about behind the know-all stegosaurus, even he was wondering if they'd ever see the finishing line again.

'You see, Lydia,' said Mr Stigson. 'There's no need to ask for directions, I've got the instincts of a homing pterodactyl.'

'You're lost, aren't you?' said Mrs Stigson.

'Dad,' said Darwin. 'Why are we sinking?'

'Swaaaaamp,' trumpeted Mrs Merrick as the mud sucked her down.

'It can't be,' flustered Mr Stigson as his knees sunk below the sludge. 'The mayor would never have signposted the route to run through a swamp.'

'Maybe somebody switched the signs,' said Dippy Egg.

Flint Beastwood trod water frantically to stop himself going under. 'I might have told you to do certain things but I never told you to do that, Dippy.'

Dippy shrugged innocently. 'Wasn't me, boss. I'm not clever enough to point signposts in the wrong direction.'

The two teams exchanged knowing glances and clutched at each other for support. 'The australopithecus!' they cried.

United against their common enemy, the dinosaurs forgot they were at war and tried desperately to save each other.

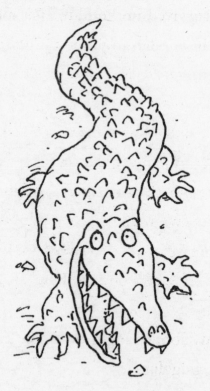

'It's all right, Phyllis, I've got you,' gurgled Mr Cretaceous as his head went under.

'Quite the contrary, I've got you, dear!' said Mrs Merrick, holding his nostrils out of the slime so he could breathe.

'Float on your backs,' gurgled Sir Tempest. 'It's how I survived in the film *Titanic Two*.'

'Can I have your autograph?' said Terry O'Dactyl as he pulled Sir Tempest to safety in the reeds.

As Frank and Ernest formed a boat with their tails, Liz Vicious made it back onto dry land along with the Stigsons. Darwin – who was the best swimmer by far – stayed in the swamp to make sure everyone was out and only hesitated when he saw Flint Beastwood floundering.

'Help! My foot's caught on a tree root. I'm drowningluglugglug.'

'Save him!' wailed Liz Vicious.

The herbivores put it to the vote. Frank and Ernest were against it because Flint had once scared their grandpa, Mrs Merrick and Sir Tempest said no good would ever come of him and, while the Stigsons wouldn't hurt a fly, they weren't about to leap back into the swamp to rescue him.

'I'll change my ways . . . Help!' gurgled Flint

just before the swamp reached his hat brim.

Darwin always looked for the good in his fellow creatures and, despite being ransomed by Flint, he decided to give him another chance and paddled across the swamp towards him.

'Come back! It's too dangerous,' called Mrs Stigson as the tyrannosaurus's head disappeared below the surface, but Darwin kept paddling until he reached Flint's hat, then he dived under.

As he disappeared too, his parents waited anxiously with their neighbours.

Three minutes.

Five.

They waited and waited. Surely no dinosaur could hold its breath for that long.

'We've lost him,' sobbed Mrs Stigson.

'Such a brave little chap,' wept Sir Tempest.

If the carnivores had turned round at that moment, they would have seen Dippy Egg dabbing his eyes, for Darwin was the only friend he had ever had.

Just when all hope had gone, the surface of the swamp broke and Darwin's head popped out, followed by Flint's. As a cheer went up, Darwin towed the spluttering, coughing tyrannosaurus back to the bank.

'Much obliged,' mumbled Beastwood, shaking the wet mud out of his hat.

'I do hope we can all live together in harmony now,' said Mr Stigson.

Flint Beastwood nodded thoughtfully. 'Harmony? We may not be singing off the same song sheet, Mr Stigson, but we can work on it.'

Darwin felt as if he'd really achieved something. To save an enemy was much harder than saving a friend but he hoped that now he'd done it, the constant threat of the carnivores to his family might stop. Nothing meant more to him than his parents and Uncle Loops.

Uncle Loops.

Darwin's heart sank. Where was Uncle Loops? In all the excitement, he assumed someone else had rescued him and that he was sitting on the bank somewhere or had fallen asleep. But he was nowhere to be seen.

'Uncle Loops? Uncle Loops?'

'Over there!' said Dippy, pointing wildly to something floating upside down in the middle of the swamp.

It was a zimmer frame.

Chapter 10

Victory

Darwin stood at the edge of the swamp and peered sadly at the handles poking out of the murky water. The rest of the frame had been sucked under and as far as anyone knew, so had Uncle Loops.

'He might still be alive,' said Darwin hopefully.

'I'm going in to save him.'

Mr Stigson dashed forward and held him back. 'It's too late, son.'

'It can't be!' wailed Darwin. 'Uncle Loops has been alive for one hundred and ninety years. He can't die!'

He pulled away from his father's grip and slipped back into the swamp.

'I'm not leaving Uncle Loops in here. In a million years time they'll find his fossilised remains and stick him in some dusty old museum. Uncle Loops *hated* museums.'

'Don't go, Darwin,' cried Mrs Stigson. 'I've already lost one son.'

Flint Beastwood stepped forward and expressed his heartfelt sympathy. 'Lost a son? That's tragic.'

Mrs Stigson jabbed him in the chest like a ninja. 'I should think you are. You were the one who ate him!'

Flint looked vaguely embarrassed. 'Are you sure it was me? I'm not the only tyrannosaurus in Raptor Road and I expect we all look the same to you.'

'Maybe we were mistaken, Lydia,' Mr Stigson muttered. 'I'm sure Mr Beastwood would have remembered eating little Livingstone.'

Mrs Stigson shot him an angry look. 'You can never just agree with me, can you Maurice? Our boy is putting his life in danger to retrieve his uncle's body and all you can do is stand there being reasonable.'

'I'm just trying to keep the peace, Lydia,' he argued.

Their argument was interrupted by Flint Beastwood taking a running jump, and diving back into the swamp. He opened his massive jaws and seized Darwin's hat with his teeth.

'See? He's going to eat our second son now!' shrieked Mrs Stigson hysterically.

But for once in his life, Beastwood did a kind and noble thing. He was a poor swimmer, he could hardly do crawl with his tiny forearms, but, being careful to avoid tree roots, his powerful legs propelled him through the water to Darwin and, though the plucky little stegosaurus protested, Flint floated him safely back to his mother.

'Beastie, you're my hero!' swooned Liz Vicious.

'Not now, Elizabeth. I have a job to do.'

The herbivores looked on in amazement as Flint turned and floated back out toward the zimmer frame.

'He's going to fetch Uncle Loops,' said Darwin softly.

'See, Lydia? He's not all bad,' said Mr Stigson.

As Flint Beastwood made repeated dives to

try and find the remains of Uncle Loops, the herbivores waited mournfully on firm ground and remembered the dear old soul.

'He was the best uncle ever,' said Darwin, his eyes brimming with tears. 'He taught me how to swim and ride my bike and spit and burp.'

Sir Tempest put a comforting arm around him. 'He was a marvellous old stick. He used to love telling his stories about the olden days, didn't he? He used to go on and on.'

'And on and on and on,' added Mrs Merrick. 'But I shall miss him terribly.'

She pulled out a handkerchief the size of a pillowcase and blew her trunk. 'It won't be the same without him.'

'Without who?'

Mrs Merrick stopped mid-parp and whisked round. 'Augustus! What the . . .? We thought you were in the swamp!'

'Flint is trying to rescue your body as we speak,' gasped Sir Tempest.

Uncle Loops parked his zimmer frame and looked bemused. 'I'm so old this body is waaaay past rescuing.'

Darwin ran over and gave Uncle Loops a hug that threatened to topple him. 'Uncle, where were you?'

'Where were *you?*' he exclaimed. 'I was following behind in the marathon and suddenly my knees locked. By the time I'd got them moving again, everyone had run off.'

'But if that's your zimmer frame, what's that thing in the swamp?' said Mrs Stigson.

The answer came back loud and clear, punctuated by a stream of very rude words.

'It's a fl★@ing b%★@!r a!★y shopping trolley!' roared Flint.

As he waded back to dry land among gales of laughter, even he saw the funny side of it. There was a lot of good-natured back-slapping. If anyone had been watching, they would have thought the herbivores and carnivores were the best of friends. In a rare moment of silence, there was a familiar giggle.

'Somebody is watching us,' snorted Mrs Merrick. 'I don't like the sound of it.'

There was a rustle in the bushes and there, dancing up and down in the nude, pulling faces and showing the whites of his eyes was . . .

'The australopithecus!'

He was furious that his signpost-switching plan had backfired and that he'd failed yet again to make the dinosaurs extinct. Nogs gnashed his teeth at them and growled.

'Ozzi, you little devil!' harrumphed Mr Stigson, waving his fist.

'After him!' yelled Flint.

The australopithecus grabbed hold of a vine and tried to swing away but it snapped, he fell and scrambled off with the dinosaurs running after him.

'He's very fast considering he's only got little legs,' puffed Uncle Loops as Ozzi zig-zagged through the trees.

'Dad almost caught up with him then,' panted

Darwin. 'He's neck and neck with Mr Beastwood. I wonder what they'll do to Ozzi if they catch him?'

He never did find out. Although both teams chased the australopithecus at top speed right out of the forest and back into the park, they lost him by the monkey bars. They weren't even distracted by Boris who was leaping up and down waving Uncle Loops's watch.

'It's a dinosaur world record!' he whooped as they thundered over the finishing line and almost bowled him over. 'Come back, chaps!' he called. 'Don't you want to know who won?'

Realising that Ozzi was beyond catching, they slowed down and made their way back to Boris. Mr Stigson was doubled-up with the effort of it all.

'I think I'm going to be sick, Lydia. I haven't run that fast since I was chased by a tyranno—'

He stopped in the middle of the word. 'Ah, well, let bygones be bygones.'

'Who won?' growled Beastwood.

Boris – who knew nothing of what had happened in the swamp – didn't like to say, although it was clear by the marks on the track that Mr Stigson had pipped Flint to the post.

'I wish I had my spectacles, Mr Beastwood,' he said. 'It was such a close thing.'

The tyrannosaurus's tiny eyes began to glint. 'I think you'll find I won, didn't I, lads?'

 The deinosuchus puffed himself up and loomed over Boris. 'Team Carnivore gets the gold,' said Mr Cretaceous. 'Unless you fancy a thump.'

The friendly tone of the afternoon was taking a rapid turn for the worse.

'I told you, Maurice,' said Mrs Stigson sighing. 'Once a carnivore, always a carnivore. They'll never change.'

Darwin folded his arms and stuck up for his father. 'Dad won! His foot went over the line first. Look, there's the imprint of his trainer.'

No sooner had he spoken than Liz Vicious sidled up to the finish line, and scrubbed out the evidence with her foot.

'Maurice,' said Boris, 'do you think you won? Only it's very hard for me to say.'

With all those wicked carnivorous eyes upon him, it was even harder for Mr Stigson. 'I think . . .' he said, as the saliva dripped from Flint's fangs, '. . . that Mr Beastwood may have beaten me by a gnat's whisker.'

'Good answer,' said Flint. 'Hear that? We've only gone and won the flaming Olympic torch!'

'Losers! Losers!' they chanted as Flint lifted the Olympic torch and paraded it round the park.

Mr Stigson sighed deeply. 'Mum's right, Darwin. Carnivores will be carnivores. We'll just have to live with it.'

As his parents walked off, Darwin stood with his uncle as the carnivores strutted about. 'That torch should have been ours, Uncle Loops.'

The old stegosaurus leant on his zimmer frame and smiled. 'Watch and learn, boy.'

Darwin watched and as Flint Beastwood climbed to the top of the slide and waved the torch triumphantly, it exploded in a shower of screaming stars and blew his hat to smithereens.

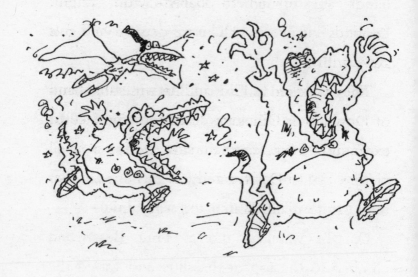

'Meteor!' screamed Flint as the cowardly carnivores ran shrieking out of the park. 'It's the end of the universe! We're going to be extinct!'

Darwin laughed as the sky lit up. 'Ozzi must have put loads of fireworks in that torch. I wouldn't want to be around when he evolves – he's cleverer than he looks.'

'But not quite as clever as me,' said Uncle Loops, wiping a trace of gunpowder off his hands. He turned to Darwin and smiled. 'Nobody kidnaps my favourite nephew and gets away with it!'

They watched as Flint and his miserable band of Downtown Dinosaurs leapt into the lake to extinguish their scorched tails. It was a small victory, but to Darwin and Uncle Loops, it was even greater than winning the Olympics.

THE UPTOWN AND DOWNTOWN PREHISTORIC SPOTTER'S GUIDE

DINOSAURS

Stegosaurus
(Steg-oh-saw-us)
Example: The Stigsons

Triceratops
(Try-sair-a-tops)
Example: Sir Tempest

Edmontonia
(Ed-mon-toe-nee-a)
Example: Boris the mayor

Ankylosaur
(Ank-ee-lo-saw)
Example: Frank
and Ernest

Mamenchisaurus
(Mah-men-chee-saw-us)
Example: Lou Gooby

Tyrannosaurus rex
(Tie-ran-o-saw-us rex)
Example: Flint Beastwood

Velociraptor
(Veh-loss-i-rap-tor)
Example: Liz Vicious

Gallimimus
(Gall-uh-my-mus)
Dippy Egg

Other Prehistoric Creatures

Deinosuchus
(Day-no-sook-us)
Example: Mr Cretaceous

Pteranodon
(Tehr-ran-oh-don)
Example: Terry
O'Dactyl

Mastadon

(Mas-tah-don)

Example: Mrs Merrick

Australopithecus

(Oss-tra-lo-pith-ah-cus)

Example: Ozzi

Cynognathus

(Sigh-nog-nay-thus)

Example: Nog

**DISCOVER THE
DOWNTOWN DINOSAURS
ONLINE!**

DOWNTOWNDINOSAURS.CO.UK

**GAMES
PUZZLES
FACT-FILES
AND MORE!**